WHERE BLOOD RUNS DEEP

EROTIC VAMPIRE PARANOMRAL

SHALA BREECE

plicit Press
Erotica Fiction

CHAPTER 1

AN INFORMAL MEETING

CHARISSE SAT QUIETLY in her father's office. She stared cross-eyed at her bangs that curled down to just above her delicate eyebrows. They were stuck together in the middle, creating an ugly part that was driving her insane. She curled her sinfully full lips and gently puffed a breath at them, hoping to unstick them without the need for actual physical labor.

She had always been a well-protected girl, spoiled rotten some would say. Still, Charisse felt that she'd never had a chance to really live, not yet. There was a deep yearning inside of her, something she just couldn't explain, and some nights she would lie in her bed simply fighting the urge to run away and abandon everything she'd ever known. It was a feeling she just didn't like. What was worse was when she tried to talk to her father; he avoided the issues. It appeared to her that there was just some deep dark secret lying between them. Sometimes it was so heavy she felt she couldn't even breathe. Looking at her bangs now, in the reflection of her phone, she gave up...

She sighed in defeat and let her eyes roam through the lavishly decorated room. Charisse never understood her father's obsession with tarnished brass and bronze. The office would have looked much more luxurious with a few pieces of sparkling silver strewn here and there. She felt somber from just sitting there.

Her mind drifted away from her musings about her father's décor. She thought about the dream she had last night, which was nearly identical to the dream from the night before and a hundred before that. Charisse's chest tightened ever so slightly.

In her dreams, Charisse would be in the throes of passion, where she was making love to a handsome, strapping man, playing out a fantasy while caressing her undulating body. Once she was sitting on a sparse mountainside, gazing up at the moon as it hung high in the night sky. Just as she was approaching her moment of bliss or contentment, something evil and malevolent would rip her from the edge.

Sometimes it was Charisse's father. Sometimes it was some dark, hideous beast, hidden in the shadows. All she could ever see were its bright, hungry eyes, burning through the darkness and into her soul. She didn't know what it meant. Maybe that is how she really saw her father; she didn't know.

A side door opened and two large men dragged a third, babbling and sobbing, by his shoulders. His feet slid across the deep, rich color of the expensive, wooden floor. After they disappeared around the corner of the hall, her father emerged through the doorway. He smiled and offered her his arms as he moved effortlessly toward her.

"Ah, Charisse, my daughter," he said, accepting her embrace with the love only a father can give to his only child.

"Another satisfied customer I see?" she smiled and slid into the chair across from his desk again.

Her father pursed his lips slightly and answered with a nod before sinking into the lavish, leather, high-back chair behind his desk. Charisse never pretended she didn't know what her father did, even if it did make her sick to her stomach from time to time. How could she be critical of him when his illegal endeavors provided so much comfort in her style of living?

Frankie Fazliani, better known as Frankie the Faz or Frankie the Fish, was the Boss of one of New York's most sinister, iron-fisted Mob rings. He was your classic "bust heads now, ask questions later" type of wise guy. Frankie was cold and calculating, vicious and ruthless, and so completely fearless that once he had his thugs wipe out an entire rival family just because his daughter was not invited to a birthday party. That was the man sitting across from Charisse right now.

Father and Daughter exchanged small-talk and Frankie made a bid to get his daughter more involved with the family business. Granted he intended on living forever but he wasn't as young as he used to be, and every new day was a bullet waiting to end his reign. He wanted her to run the show when he was gone but Charisse didn't show much interest in it.

"Good night dad," she said, leaning over to give him a peck on the cheek before heading off for the night.

Frankie rubbed his eyes and watched her leave. He traced his tongue along the edge of his teeth and wondered if she would ever be like him. Under different circumstances, he'd be fine with her not wanting to run the family business, but she was his daughter after all. It was in her blood to follow in his footsteps.

Charisse flashed a wink at the seedy-looking henchman that guarded her apartment door. She thought it was cute how her father was so over-protective but she was well aware of his motivation to have such ways. It wasn't like Frankie didn't own the top three floors of the tower. Charisse didn't get as much as a blink from the guy. She gave her long, raven hair a sensuous flip as she passed and closed the door behind her.

After discarding her clothes and pulling on just a black, silk robe before getting into the shower, Charisse walked into the kitchen to pour a glass of wine. She paused at the large windows and gazed out at the city skyline. New York City was nothing short of stunning at night. Her sparkling eyes lifted from the city to the unusually bright, full moon.

She could almost see every nook and cranny of its surface. It was beautiful and hung nestled gently between a million pinpoints of light. Charisse felt herself drawn to it as if it called to her like a lover. Her large brown eyes followed every contour and she felt her chest rise and fall deeply with each passing moment.

"Where are you?" she whispered then felt a familiar tingle dance up her spine.

Charisse pressed her hand against the glass and caressed the outline of the moon while she brushed the back of her hand down her neck and between her large, pillowy breasts. The touch of her hand through the silk forced her eyes closed for a moment. There were so many things in her life that she hadn't experienced because of who her father was. Being with a man was one of them.

There were no dates, no handsome man holding her hand while walking through the park, no love or lust. It was only her and her father and his goons. She desired to be held and loved tenderly by a rugged, loving man. Perhaps she was just a romantic at heart, but she burned to give into the desire that boiled inside of her.

Charisse slowly untied her robe and let it drop from her shoulders. She stood there in all her naked glory, staring into eternity and wondering where her place was in the world and if she would really find love. She hated the fact that she'd spend another night alone, like the night before and the night before that.

She placed her hands on the window and pressed her soft breasts against its cool, smooth surface, feeling the heat of the night coursing through her body again, as it had every night for the past year. It was like a starving animal inside of her, clawing its way out in search of something to satisfy her cravings. She growled herself, in total frustration. Her insides felt like molten lava spooling through her veins. She ran her hands through her hair, not knowing where else to put them.

Even if Charisse couldn't find love then maybe lust would suffice. Lust. Pure, animalistic lust. She rubbed her breasts against the glass and ran her tongue along its surface. She felt the desire stirring deep inside of her, begging to be released. She moaned against the glass and ran her slender hands over her curvaceous, creamy ass. The musk of her overpowering arousal began to fill her pulsing nostrils.

It was the most intense craving she had felt in months and the inferno that burned deep in her succulent, virgin flower threatened to consume her. Slowly Charisse turned around and leaned against the cool glass. She covered an erect nipple with the palm of her hand and gently dug the tips of her fingers into her supple breast. Her other hand traveled across her smooth, flat stomach and inched toward the source of her heat.

Her hips moved gently and she squeezed her eyes shut

when her fingers found her sensitive nub, partly nestled within her silky flesh. Charisse parted her creamy thighs gently and growled in need as she moved her fingers deftly between her moistening, womanly folds. She was so hot that she could have ravished the thug keeping watch outside of her door and there would have been no stopping her.

Maybe that was what she needed to satisfy her carnal cravings. Maybe she didn't need to make love to a life partner. Maybe she just needed a good fuck. As the fantasies swirled through her mind, she delicately pressed her fingers deep into her dripping wet flesh. She loved how it felt to pleasure itself, as it was like some innate ability she had been blessed with. She always knew exactly where to stroke to hit the right spot too. Her girlfriends always conceded to her that they did the same thing but were unable to orgasm themselves.

She supposed she was just one of those super-sensitive women, the kind that needed a good pounding and enjoyed more touching than others. She could feel her pleasures building and she dove deeper, every time pulling away with more juices following in her fingers' wake. She would have gotten the fake dildo that one of her girlfriends had bought for her as a joke, but she couldn't stop. She didn't want to.

"Mmmmm," she groaned as she added a second.

She eased her fingers in and out of her quickly and determinedly, pleasing her in the same fashion they had several times a week. Her hot pussy cried in agony as she pulled her fingers from inside and lifted them to her lips. Slowly she slid them into her mouth and moaned at the taste of her own juices. Finally, she pulled her saliva-soaked fingers from her wet mouth and took several deep breaths.

Charisse swallowed hard and scooped up her robe

before disappearing into her bedroom. Whatever it was that called to her like an anguished ghost had started a fire deep inside of her. She retired to her bedroom in hopes of fending off the creature but knew that eventually the animal in her would win out.

CHAPTER 2

AFTERNOON DELIGHTS

TWO WEEKS PASSED and Charisse's father noticed her becoming more irritable and angry. Several times Frankie tried to sit her down and hunt for the root of her troubles, but each time she just blew him off. Today, however, he decided not to pry and looked at her with as loving eyes as he could.

"Gimme a sec," he told her then pulled out his cellphone.

Frankie mashed his thick, calloused fingers into his cellphone and waited impatiently. He remembered a time cellular phones didn't exist. It wasn't that technology evolved too fast for him. It just seemed that as things became more high-tech they became more cumbersome and prone to malfunction.

"Porky, it's Frankie," he said to the goon on the other end of the call.

"Take today off," Frankie ordered then thumbed the call off.

Charisse's eyes lit up. She couldn't believe it and found herself in shock. Her father had called his goons off for once. Frankie nodded then pulled out a small pistol from his desk drawer. At first, Charisse was going to resist but decided that if her father was going to call off the Goon Squad, she could at least make the compromise and it wasn't like she hadn't carried a gun before.

Frankie watched his daughter in complete silence as she took the pistol and tucked it away in her tiny purse. It was time to let her experience life without his constant protection. He trusted her and hoped she could protect herself. Time would tell whether or not his trust would be misplaced.

Hours later, Charisse basked in the afternoon sun as she waited patiently for *him*. Unbeknownst to her father, she had met a young man months ago. He was handsome and caring and most importantly, he didn't care that she was the daughter of a ruthless mob boss. They had only met a handful of times before. She didn't want to risk getting ratted out by her father's thugs, but this time the worry was gone.

But each time they met was more magical than the last. In her heart, she felt Donovan was different. So different than anyone she had ever met before that she swore he could be the one. And now with her looser reigns, she had the opportunity to explore their relationship.

"Charisse, mi amore," Donovan said, leaning down and placing a gentle kiss on her smooth, bare shoulder.

Charisse popped up from the park bench, wrapped her arms around him, and drew him in. Their lips met in furious passion. She pressed herself against him, feeling the firmness of his muscular chest against her through the sheer fabric of her dress. She needed him badly and hoped that Donovan could handle the storm of frustration she'd unleash upon him.

Hand-in-hand, Charisse, and Donovan walked through Central Park on their way to his place. They talked a little here and there as they enjoyed each other's company. Donovan seemed a bit surprised when she told him how her father called off his thugs to let her actually have a life. He'd heard stories about Frankie and the mob boss didn't seem like the kind to let his daughter gallivant around without someone protecting her.

"Maybe he wants you to appreciate his protectiveness," Donovan said as they walked.

"I know. I understand where he's coming from," she replied. Her voice held a touch of contempt in it.

"I'm almost 23. I want him to know I can make good decisions and take care of myself," Charisse continued.

The truth was, she hadn't really thought of the consequences of not having her father's goons around watching over her. The desire to do what she wanted without her every move being reported back to Frankie had blinded her to the reality of her life as a mobster's child. But she was with Donovan now and she felt safer than she'd ever felt before.

"I'm sure you can handle yourself," he said with a mischievous wink and then a little pat on her rear.

Charisse purred and nuzzled against him, growing impatient. She wondered if today would be the day Donovan took her. She'd been yearning for it since they'd met though she realized that back then it wasn't about being with Donovan, it was about satisfying her sexual frustration.

Now, however, it was different. She didn't look at Donovan and see a slab of meat with a penis. She truly cared for him, maybe even loved him, and wasn't afraid to show him just how much either. Today, for the first time, the notion of her inexperience with men crept into her brain.

Charisse wasn't sure if it was that or the sweet excitement of anticipation. She watched plenty of pornographic videos over the years of having to satisfy her own urges and she had learned quite a bit from them. She was quite confident that she knew enough to satisfy Donovan. All she could do was wait and see.

Finally, they were at his place, a meager apartment that looked very much like her father's office. It was quaint but dull. Charisse smiled politely and told him she loved it. Donovan returned her smile and eyed her slowly from head to toe. She could feel the desperate heat in his stare and resisted the urge to pounce on him and use him every which way she could.

She sat quietly on the couch and watched him pour some wine. It was complete and utter torture. Charisse had waited for so long for this moment and Donovan knew it. He purposely took his time. He wanted to tease her, to make her hotter until she was about to burst, then and only then would he take her to his bed. He wanted her to ache for him and only him.

Donovan knew she had never made love to a man before. He also knew of her deliciously dirty self-pleasuring sessions, how there were days she refused to get out of bed because she was so aroused that she couldn't keep her hands off her yearning, young body. He had spent many nights lying awake in bed, knowing she was home, covered in a light sheen of sweat, moaning in ecstasy as she fought to quell the hunger inside of her.

Donovan would close his eyes and imagine he was with her, plunging himself deep into her burning lust, and then in that one powerful moment, he would climax with her.

His seed would burst from his hard, throbbing manhood and splatter across his chiseled abs as he imagined filling her silky, moist depths with each lustful spurt.

Donovan glanced over at her on the couch as he corked the bottle of wine. The thought of it was arousing him now. His swollen length pressed against the fly of his jeans and begged to feel her warm, wet flesh around it.

When Donovan joined her on the couch, Charisse was waiting with the hungriest eyes he had ever seen. His growing bulge pulled her gaze to the front of his pants and teased her sensitive nipples to strain through her bra and the flimsy fabric of her sundress. She was done waiting.

Donovan handed her a glass of wine and watched her place it on the coffee table before sliding to her knees. She crawled fluidly toward him, like a cat stalking its prey. Donovan watched her with growing anticipation as she crawled between his knees. They both knew what was coming and Donovan simply leaned back against the couch and watched.

Charisse could feel the wetness of her panties brush the apex of her smooth, supple inner thighs. She stopped herself from reaching down and running her fingers over her sweet, burning folds like she had done a thousand times before. It was almost embarrassing that she was so used to pleasing herself that in the presence of Donovan, she automatically thought of her fingers instead of him.

After struggling against the raging inferno that burned inside of her, Charisse had Donovan's pants off and her fingers firmly wrapped around the girth of his shaft. She stared at his thick, pulsing manhood in amazement. She'd seen a hundred in her erotic movies and on the internet but she had never seen one in real life, let alone touched one.

Charisse began to tremble slightly as she nervously guided his swollen glans to her moist, pouting lips.

She nibbled on its spongy tip, teasing it with her lips and teeth before running her wet tongue along the tiny seam beneath. Donovan hissed in delight but made no move to urge her further. He wanted her to satisfy him at her own pace. Soon his swollen head slipped past her full, inviting lips as she sunk her juicy mouth down on his raging shaft.

Charisse moaned through her flaring nostrils as she worked his rock-hard length in and out of her mouth, slowly at first then more furiously as her mouth relaxed further to take his size in. She didn't know how long he could handle it and left it up to him to stop her just short of reaching his peak, or not. Charisse was so enthralled with pleasing him that if he chose to fill her warm, wet mouth with his juice then she'd happily take every succulent drop.

She cupped and massaged his silky balls gently as she sucked his cock like an expert. Her fingers danced over his hard flesh as her lips traveled the length of his manhood. Having felt this day would come, she would practice with her dildo at home, perfecting her oral stimulation as she bided her time.

Donovan moaned and nearly dropped his glass of wine on the couch. He was expecting her to be reckless and full of energy but he'd never experienced a woman sucking him with such voracity as Charisse was. She took him fast and deep, shoving the excess of his pulsating meat down her eager, tightening throat. He literally drooled at the thought of her fucking him with the same sinful abandonment.

After just a few minutes of her adept pleasure, her jaw muscles began to ache. She let his swollen member pop from her tired mouth. It glistened with her saliva and pulsed in need. Seeing its subtle call for more stirred something inside of her, something powerful and animalistic.

Suddenly all of her wants and desires came crashing through her like a terrible thunderstorm of lust. All of her visions and fantasies of making love to Donovan twisted into something darker and more primitive. The wanton look in her eyes melted away from the pure, sizzling lust that threatened to burn Donovan to a crisp.

With a guttural growl, Charisse ripped open his shirt, shooting a myriad of defenseless buttons every which way. She clawed at his chiseled abs and ripped chest. She traced every curve of his powerful muscles and reveled in their tightness and strength. She tried to contain the blinding desire that welled up in her young, tender body.

She wanted to take it slow, she tried to, but she couldn't. The sexual beast inside of her had been awakened and demanded to be satisfied despite her fleeting self-control. Charisse dropped her dress to the floor and climbed onto him without removing her panties or bra. Charisse pulled her soaked, lacy thong to the side and guided Donovan's throbbing head to her warm, buttery folds.

Donovan held his breath and waited for the moment they had ached for so long. Charisse lowered herself and buried his rock-hard length completely inside of her. She arched her smooth, contoured back and tilted her head, feeling herself completely filled by a man for the first time. She held her pose for several moments as she choked out several moans of desire.

Slowly she reached back and unclasped her bra, letting it fall onto Donovan's lap and freeing her ample, round breasts to him. Her hands slid up her smooth, flat stomach then cupped and squeezed her pillowy breasts. She felt her taut, sensitive nipples pressing hard against her palms as she dug her fingers roughly into her soft flesh.

After an eternity, Charisse dropped against Donovan. She pressed her hot tits against his powerfully muscled chest and kissed him deeply. Their moist tongues swirled hungrily together through the heat of their sinful desire. Donovan moved his strong hands down her creamy, smooth back and over her soft, round ass.

Charisse's head spun from the euphoria of their lust and when Donovan's powerful fingers dug into her fleshy cheeks, she howled into his mouth as her intense hunger took over. She started pounding her hips desperately against his lap. Charisse's body writhed wildly against Donovan as she drove his cock into her starving pussy like a wrecking ball.

Donovan thrust his hips to meet her movements. She moved like an insatiable animal, wild and reckless, free from her father's bonds, and intent on quenching the abyssal thirst she had harbored her entire life. Donovan's world fell away into the darkness, leaving just them, alone, and fucking vehemently on the couch.

Their powerful, lusting moans echoed through Donovan's apartment. He had surely bitten off more than he could chew. He expected hours of lovemaking, tender and tedious while they explored each other slowly, surely not the carnal heat threatening to ignite the entire building. He wasn't complaining.

His hands slid from her supple skin and dug into the couch's cushions. His knuckles strained white as he held on for his life as Charisse reared back and started impaling herself even harder on his angry meat. She wailed hauntingly and her eyes rolled back into her head as she felt the deep, intense pang of her orgasm racing to the rim of her being. Then it hit her.

Her bursting pussy clenched around Donovan's cock like a terrible vice. It gripped his throbbing shaft and milked him hard and fast, begging it to erupt deep inside of her and add his crescendo to hers. Donovan tried to hold back for as long as he could but the slick, tight pumping of her ravenous grip dragged him over the edge with her.

Charisse growled at the top of her lungs as she rode the crest of her orgasm and felt Donovan's steaming, thick juices explode deep inside of her, flooding her quivering quim with every drop she could milk. Every desire she had ever felt, every fantasy she had ever imagined, every wish she had ever made came crashing down on them in a moment of blissful heat and launched them beyond the clouds.

They collapsed together in a tangle of flesh and gasps. Charisse trembled in Donovan's cradling arms as she fought to recover from the most powerful experience of her life. She nuzzled her face into the nape of his neck and submitted to her sudden fatigue.

As he tenderly stroked her sweaty cheek, Donovan wondered what he had gotten himself into or even more so, what he had gotten Charisse into. Frankly, he never expected this day to come and hadn't considered the repercussions. She was a part of his life now and he struggled inside as to whether or not to tell her who he really was.

The next morning, Frankie pounded on his daughter's apartment door. Charisse groaned and rolled over in bed then cracked her heavy eyelids to glare at the clock. The red LEDs said 9:17 AM, not late but not too early, and yet it seemed like hours earlier than it really was. She hadn't come home until well after midnight, and two more sessions of heat and passion with Donovan had bled her strength.

Even though her lust seemed sated, she had the dream again. She stood before a wall of darkness and tried to peer beyond its surface. There was nothing, nothing at all. Then those eyes, those bright, burning eyes, appeared and struck her with excruciating fear and intense wonder. She could hear the beast's labored, ragged breath as it hungered for something.

Charisse turned and ran, trying to escape the void that moved as swiftly as she. She felt something tear across the hem of her flowing skirt. She looked back in terror and caught a glimpse of a hideous claw retreating into the pitch that followed her. It was disturbing, very disturbing. But it was morning now and the beast was gone. Despite her best efforts to ignore her father, she rolled over and groaned.

"Charisse!" Frankie growled from the other side of the door.

He waited patiently for his daughter to answer. In the entire world, only she could get away with making him wait. Anyone else would have had their door bashed in and their life was stolen for the sake of Frankie's impatience.

"What?" Charisse said sleepily as she opened the door.

"Get dressed and come to my office now," he said angrily. "It's time you decide once and for all if you are in or not."

Charisse watched her father stalk away and frowned. She knew this day would come and wasn't sure if she could handle it or if she wanted to. She slipped on a pair of sweats and a tank top, tied her long hair into a messy ponytail, and left. The thoughts of Donovan that lingered in her head gave way to dread and wonder. Charisse held her breath as she entered her father's office and opened the door to his *conference* room.

She was greeted by a man gagged and strapped to a chair. His wild eyes bulged in pain and begged her to help him. His fear was rank and thick on her tongue and Charisse's stomach threatened to turn. She could hear his heart pounding a million times a second.

Frankie met his daughter with a kiss on the cheek. She eyed the hammer in his hand dubiously and connected the dots. The poor fellow's hand has strapped a piece of wood attached to the arm of the chair. He tried to curl his fingers beneath the pressure and shook his head violently.

"Charisse will teach you your first lesson," Frankie said to the bawling man and extended the handle of the hammer to his daughter.

"What lesson?" she asked. She knew the power she held over her father. There were a handful of *family* members who could get away with that question. She was one of them and the only one there.

"Little Mike here needs to be reminded of his place within the organization," Frankie said, not seeing the need to explain further, even to his own daughter.

"Remind him, will ya?" Frankie nodded to the hammer in his hand.

Charisse curled her fingers around the wooden handle. Her nostrils flared as she watched Little Mike squirm against his bonds. He looked familiar, but couldn't place his face. As the hammer fell, she remembered. He lived in Donovan's apartment building.

The hammer smashed into his pinky finger. Little Mike's eyes nearly popped out and he screamed into the gag.

"You follow *my* orders, you see," Frankie spat at him and nodded to Charisse.

She crushed the hammer into his ring finger. Little Mike screamed in agony. The hideous snap of his bones echoed through Charisse's ears. Her chest heaved with the power that suddenly overtook her body. There was a dark satisfaction in torturing this poor fellow for whatever transgression he made against her father.

Her father started to speak but Little Mike's muffled wailing cut him off as Charisse swung the hammer with both hands and obliterated his middle finger. Blood splattered across the wooden plank and she could smell the pain that screamed through the thug's body.

"You like that?" Charisse growled and pushed the bloody head of the hammer under Little Mike's chin. She peered into his eyes with venom and contempt. Something was taking its hold on her, pushing her to embrace the darkness hidden inside of her.

Suddenly those eyes flooded her mind again. She reeled at the satisfaction that burned so brightly from those eyes that she closed her own. Her chest heaved in shock as the image in her mind zoomed out and she finally saw the beast face to face. It was her.

She was naked. Blood covered her mouth and cheeks and trickled in long sinuous lines down her body. Her fingers were hideously crooked with long, thick nails that dripped blood too. Her image simply smiled at her with a nod.

Frankie stood by silently with his arms folded across his chest, watching Charisse come into her own as a member of their ring and more importantly, as his daughter. He glanced to the thug guarding the door. The bulky man arched a brow and nodded his approval slowly. They were all happily caught off guard by Charisse's sudden flavor of violence.

"You gonna cross my father again?" she asked darkly.

Little Mike whimpered uncontrollably and shook his head. His eyes begged her to believe him. The power of his fear drove the truth of his confession into her chest like a rough wooden spike. She believed him. Charisse nodded and started to withdraw, satisfied with the torture she put Little Mike through.

Almost satisfied, she crushed his index finger with the hammer uncontrollably, several times until his digit looked like ground meat. When she was done, Charisse smiled sweetly at her father. Now she was satisfied and tossed the hammer onto a small table in the corner. She kissed her father on the cheek and asked him to join her for breakfast in her apartment when he was finished.

Frankie nodded with a proud smile and watched his daughter go. He sensed something in her, something dark and malicious, burning to come to light. He thought it was time to reveal his darkest secret, one he had harbored her entire life. Breakfast seemed like the perfect opportunity.

CHAPTER 3

REVELATIONS

CHARISSE SAT CURLED up on her couch and silently stared at the moon. The shock of her father's words from breakfast haunted her. She had always felt something was different about her but she refused to believe what her father had confessed.

For the first time in a long time, she was able to look at the moon without the intense draw of lust that usually ended with her masturbating long and hard to appease her hunger. Did she subconsciously accept her father's admission and satisfy the beast within or was it that she was so distracted that she didn't notice it? Charisse couldn't decide.

She absently picked up a tiny vanity mirror and looked at herself. Charisse rolled her head from side to side and bared her teeth. They looked normal enough. None were more elongated or sharper than the others. If what Frankie had told her really was true, why hadn't she ever seen him as what he really was? She needed to go out and then nabbed her cell phone to call Donovan.

"What's wrong?" he asked. She never called him at night.

"I'll explain when I see you. I just need to be somewhere besides here," she replied.

Donovan gave her a corner to meet him. Although Frankie had given her a bit more freedom than before, they weren't ready to be seen together too close to Charisse's apartment building. Charisse tugged on her heavy trench coat over her t-shirt and sweats and left her apartment to meet with Donovan.

It took her a block or so before she realized what she was wearing and the absence of anticipation for meeting with the man that had so quickly took her heart. Charisse's lips bent into a frown. She should have gotten dressed up in something sexy for her man. Her tight, lavender dress would have been nice. It left most of her back exposed and she normally loved the way the stretchy fabric hugged her large breasts and round hips.

Today she was just out of it. Certainly distracted by what her father had admitted to her, Charisse found herself free of her usual routine. It bothered her somewhat and wondered if this is how it would be. She desperately hoped Donovan would understand and offer some words of comfort.

"Hey," Donovan said as he strolled up to her on the corner.

"Hey," she said distractingly.

"You okay? What's up?"

Charisse forced a smile and looped her arm in Donovan's. They walked without any particular destination in mind as she told him about breakfast with her father. Donovan listened intently but offered nothing in response and that irritated her a little.

When she was done with her story, Donovan simply kissed her on the top of the head and walked silently beside her. They crossed a few streets and meandered down a few alleys as if they were going somewhere now. Charisse didn't care where they were going. She felt safe with Donovan even if he wasn't giving her the response she desired.

As they approached a corner, the deep thrust of music touched Charisse's body and vibrated through her chest. She lifted her head from Donovan's arm and looked up at him. He smiled.

"I think it's what you need," he said.

"I'm not in the mood to the club," she protested lightly.

"Trust me, okay?"

She did. Donovan led her around the corner and then one more after that before stopping at what looked like a run-down, vacant apartment or office building. The music was coming from deep inside the structure and there were no visible signs to indicate the name of the place.

A large, burly man opened a door to allow them to pass. Once inside, the music was deafening. The constant boom-boom assaulted Charisse's ears and pounded through her head. Donovan led her through a series of hallways and stairwells then finally out onto a small balcony that over-looked the dance floor.

"What is this place?" Charisse asked him.

"It's the place you need to be," he answered cryptically then looked at his watch. "We're just in time too."

Charisse looked at her own watch. It was a few minutes before 1:00 AM. She counted the seconds with her watch and when it turned one, the music stopped, leaving a loud ring echoing through her ears.

"You know what time it is?" the DJ shouted to the dance floor.

Hundreds of men and women howled and hooted then began stomping their feet. The music gonged and then slowly turned into an irritating hum. Finally, it ended in a clash of symbols and then exploded into a tribal beat.

Donovan could feel Charisse's heart pounding in her chest as she tightened her grip on his arm. Together they watched as the audience slowly dropped to all fours as their forms melted into something grotesque. Charisse jumped and looked up at Donovan.

His eyes had changed. They were bright yellow, like a beast, like the ones she saw in her dreams. Charisse slowly backed away from him. The fear welled up inside of her and tried to choke the breath from her lungs.

"It's okay," Donovan said as he extended his hand to her. "This is who *we* are."

"They're all," Charisse tried to say the word but couldn't.

"Werewolves?" he finished for her. "Yes. Them, me, you, your father. All of us are."

Then a sudden peace overcame Charisse. She felt as if she were floating in the clouds. The feeling wrapped its warm, tender arms around her and guided her to the edge of the balcony. She stared at her brethren in wonder and amazement. For the first time since she could remember, Charisse felt like she truly belonged.

Hours later, Charisse and Donovan were curled up together on the couch in his apartment. He ran his fingers through her hair gently as they talked. Charisse had a hundred questions to ask him and a hundred more after that and she tried her best not to sound like she was interrogating him.

"So covens are like classes or castes, right?" she asked, thinking she understood his explanation.

"Yeah," he said. "Your father's so-called *family* is made up of several covens. You and he belong to the highest one. The rest of us do as we are told when it comes to *family* business."

Charisse shifted her head on Donovan's chest slightly and listened to his heartbeat. She closed her eyes and remembered the last time she was here with her lover. She had been overwhelmed by the urges that seemed so distant now. She recalled how much she had needed him and the rawness of the heat between them.

As she relived that afternoon, she felt the familiar stirrings start to spark inside of her. Familiar but different. She wanted Donovan again, but there was tenderness in her desire this time. She wanted to feel his body against hers as they moved as one, blissfully making love. That's what she wanted. She wanted to truly make love to Donovan and not just some hollow, unmoving fuck fest.

Donovan caressed her back through her t-shirt and closed his eyes as she explored all the contours of his muscular chest. Charisse pressed herself harder against him as she slid her hand up under his shirt. The firmness of his muscles beneath her touch kindled the fire inside of her. She curled her leg around his and pressed her pelvis against it.

Charisse cooed softly at the gentle shocks of pleasure that radiated through her body and filled her with a sense of erotic warmth. She felt a hunger slowly building inside of her. It was much different than the last time she was with Donovan and he could sense it too. This was the moment they had both really been looking forward to.

She lifted his shirt and placed a myriad of butterfly kisses on his toned chest. Donovan shifted slightly on the couch, slouching a bit so he could dip his fingers just under the waistband of her sweat pants and caress her silky, supple skin. She inhaled sharply and trembled slightly beneath his touch.

Charisse's tongue circled languidly around Donovan's aroused nipple. She ground her moistening mound against his leg more urgently. She knew he was getting the hint; no man could be that dense. It was frustrating her and she wondered what he really wanted.

Did he want the heartfelt passion that swelled inside of her like rolling waves or did he prefer that aggressive, mindless slut that simply fucked him with every ounce of pent-up anger and frustration from two weeks ago? Donovan wasn't capitalizing on her growing desire. Charisse glanced up at him.

Donovan's head was tilted back on the couch and his eyes were closed tightly. He seemed to be enjoying the moment as she should have been. She decided that maybe he just wanted to feel her passion and desire for as long as he could before they retired to his bedroom. Charisse returned her attention to his smooth chest and nipped at his tight skin. She'd be happy either way.

Donovan slid his hand further beneath her sweatpants and panties. Her luscious cheeks felt deliciously soft as he groped her round, tender, young ass. Charisse moaned softly and pressed back against his squeezing hand. His touch was delicate but powerful.

She kissed up his chest to the front of his neck. He squirmed at the touch of her supple lips on his skin as she suckled along his neck to the side. The heat was building inside of her, driving her to grind against his leg harder, rubbing her swollen nub against his solid leg. She could feel the wetness of her soaked panties against her smooth, bare flesh.

Charisse fought to contain herself. She was quickly losing control and told herself to take it slow or she would end up a feverish mess like last time. She let her hand loll gently toward Donovan's crotch. He took in a breath and held it in anticipation. He was just as hungry as she was, perhaps even more, but hid it much better.

"I love you," she whispered into his ear before sucking his lobe into her wet mouth.

Donovan was about to whisper his love too until Charisse's fingers closed around his hard, throbbing manhood and started to stroke him gently through his pants. He groaned lightly as she delicately took his earlobe between her teeth and tugged on it playfully. The shoe was on the other foot this time. This time it was Charisse that was intent on making Donovan want her more than anything in the world.

Her hips circled slowly against his leg, keeping perfect rhythm with the movement of her hand over his slacks. Charisse inhaled slowly, breathing in the scent of Donovan's desire. It fueled the flames that started to consume her inside. Then she stopped.

Charisse slid off the couch and smiled seductively at Donovan. His hungry eyes were glued to her. She ran her hands slowly down her cheeks and neck then the top that concealed her large, soft breasts. She squeezed them gently and whimpered. Charisse massaged her chest firmly before slowly lifting her top up over her head.

Her hard, sensitive nipples strained against her white lace bra. Donovan's mouth watered as he imagined drawing them between his lips. Charisse playfully tossed her shirt at him and drew her hands slowly down her body. Her hips swayed sensually to the tune in her head. She spun in slow circles as she worked for her hands inside her sweatpants and began to slide them over her hips.

With her back to Donovan, she slid her pants further. The top of her white lace thong teased him. He imagined the soft fabric disappearing deeply between her scrumptious cheeks. He was dimly aware that he was rubbing his aching member through his slacks as he watched, completely enthralled, as Charisse drew her pants even further down then kicked them errantly away.

She shot in a sultry smile over her shoulder and saunter off toward his bedroom. Donovan sat still, frozen in place as he watched her tender ass sway gently with each step. He couldn't wait to join her. When she disappeared through the doorway, he rose from the couch. His throbbing shaft bulged beneath the fabric of his slacks, begging to penetrate her silky smooth flower.

Charisse's panties and bra flew through the doorway and landed on the floor in front of him. He picked them up and pressed them against his face. Donovan inhaled her musky scent from her slimy panties then quickly stripped out of his clothes and disappeared into the bedroom.

When Donovan entered the room, Charisse was waiting patiently for him. She was on her hands and knees on the bed near the edge with her head down submissively. She wanted him to take her, however, he wanted. Soft and slow, hard and ruthless, it didn't matter to her. The moment he entered her she knew she would lose control.

She moaned softly at the grip of his hands on her hips. Donovan guided his swollen glans to her silky, glistening folds and entered her. Charisse dug her fingers into the bed in ecstasy as their night of passion-filled love-making began.

CHAPTER 4

FAMILY BUSINESS

THE NEXT AFTERNOON found Charisse in the back of her father's stretched limousine. Frankie sat across from his daughter with his window cracked slightly and nursed his cigar. They didn't seem to be going anywhere in particular so she figured they were going to have a *talk*.

"I heard you were at the Wolves' Den last night," Frankie said pointedly.

"You got your goons following me again?" Her tone was laced with a touch of venom. She hadn't come home until just before sunrise and hid her puffy, sleepless eyes behind her large, dark sunglasses. Frankie just shook his head.

"Obviously someone took you there and I'm sure you were told exactly what the place was," he started. Frankie tried not to sound condescending.

"Gossip, dear," her father continued. "It's not every day that my daughter goes there."

Charisse wanted to clam up. After a night of shock and sensuous love-making, she was having her doubts about whether or not she was fully accepting the truth. Her father held something back from her, he always did, but for the life's sake, she couldn't figure out what it was. It gnawed at her like a starving dog would gnaw on a bare bone.

"So who's the guy?" she spat while struggling to stay awake.

"Charisse, I honestly don't care," Frankie said to her surprise. "I'm more concerned with your role in our family."

"I know, dad," she said.

Charisse knew what her responsibilities to her father were and wanted to get more involved but she had been rather distracted. The *example* she had made with Little Mike wasn't as bad as she thought. The moment she stepped foot into that room, a feeling of dread had come over her. When she was finished, she felt a twisted sense of satisfaction.

Now that she had a little closure with her newly revealed origin and her lustful cravings for sex had subsided, she felt that she could really dedicate herself to Frankie's will. Charisse slowly removed her sunglasses and looked at her father. He was waiting patiently for her to continue.

"I've been messed up for a while," she explained, "but I think I'm ready now."

"Good!" her father smiled and tapped the window between them and the driver.

They sat in silence as the driver steered them to an unknown destination. Charisse wondered what her father had up his sleeve. Everything he did and said had a purpose. It appeared he had already planned something for them. The anticipation was building inside of her and she felt that familiar pull from the unknown.

It whispered to her that she could handle whatever her father had planned. It held her in its gentle grasp, comforting her and giving her strength. It was intoxicating and Charisse admitted to herself that she missed it. She didn't fully realize the void that had been left in her after that afternoon with Donovan. Truly the beast inside of her wanted its attention.

After a few turns, the car glided to a stop. The door opened and a rather slim, business-like man stepped into the limo with them. He was clean-cut and dressed like a banker. Charisse gave him a sideways glance before the door closed and they were on their way again.

Frankie introduced the stranger to his daughter as one Mr. Troy Langfork. The nature of his relationship with her father wasn't exactly revealed to her, just that he represented some people whom her father did business with. They rode for what seemed like the entire afternoon while she listened to her father and Mr. Langfork haggle over details of a deal that was supposed to go down in a few days.

"So exactly what cut do you get?" Frankie asked.

"Not that it's your business but I'm well compensated," Troy replied.

Charisse was surprised at his sudden attitude toward her father. Throughout their entire business dealing, he had remained poised and very diplomatic toward Frankie's demands. Her father, on the other hand, seemed quite content with the sarcasm. Maybe the stranger had earned just enough respect to get a pass for that.

"So then 250 large, off the top, is pretty standard?"

Charisse's father's question bleached the man's face and made his jaw tremble. Her eyes darted back and forth between the two. It was an interesting twist.

"I spoke to your employer this morning," Frankie said.

He reached into his jacket and pulled out his heat. Troy's eyes widened and frantically looked around for a route of escape. There was none. Frankie crushed the barrel of his pistol into the slender man's mouth then a second time for good measure.

"He was confused why I said that 1.75 mil was a reasonable price," Frankie said while screwing the silencer into the end of the gun. "He thought the deal was for 1.5. Yet, the entire time we've talked, you've been spouting 1.75. Why is that?"

"My- my mistake," Troy stammered with a bloody mouth.

"We discussed previous deals too," her father said, shaking his head. "You should've taken your cheese and left while you could."

Before the man could say another word, Frankie lifted his gun quickly and pulled the trigger. Everything seemed to move in slow motion to Charisse's eyes. She watched as the bullet crossed the dozen or so inches between her father's gun and Troy's head. The stranger's face twisted quickly in fear just before the bullet penetrated his forehead.

Charisse jumped and shielded her face with her hand as the side of Troy's head exploded. Blood and brain tissue blasted her and she glared at her father with wild eyes. Frankie simply unscrewed the silencer and put it and his gun away as if nothing had happened at all. Business as usual.

"Dad! Fuck!" Charisse yelled at him. "A little warning would have been nice."

He looked at his daughter. Her angry stare left him to survey the damage to her clothes. On the outside, she seemed more upset that her relatively new outfit was ruined than to the fact her father just murdered some guy that was sitting right next to her. But inside, inside was a different story.

Charisse felt the animal in her stir again and the pang of lust that wracked her body. She closed her eyes for a moment to try and focus. She felt it seeping into her every pore, like before, like before Donovan and the years before him. Raw, unbridled lust began burning its way out.

"Charisse," Frankie said before she cut him off.

"Take me home," she growled and curled her legs up on the seat.

Before the door even closed behind her, Charisse bolted to the bathroom. She twisted on the shower then looked at herself in the mirror.

"What do you want?" she screamed at her reflection.

The ride home had been grueling. She fought the urge to touch herself. Her entire body lusted for her. Her nipples anxiously begged her to touch them and her pussy cried out in pure, dark desire. Coming home only seemed to make it worse.

"What?" she screamed again before doubling over in a dry-heaving fit.

Charisse collapsed on the floor. The tile was cold and smooth against her naked body. She sobbed and eased her hand between her smooth, trembling thighs. Her body responded to her touch as she gently stroked her hard, sensitive nub, but her mind was blind to the pleasure.

Her tears pooled on the hard floor while she cried. Her thoughts swam with questions. Why was this happening to her? What perverted force could possibly have such a strong grasp on her and why did it insist on ravaging her with lust? Charisse would have preferred pain or anguish over the bestial appetite that drove her uncontrollably to crave sex in any form.

As her crying faded to whimpering and then finally ceased, she was overcome by the intense pleasure that grappled her body. She realized she was lying on the floor and furiously pumping two fingers deeply past her dripping wet, silky folds. The lust raged through her, making her hungrier with each automatous thrust.

Charisse began to think about Donovan and the beautiful night they had together last night. As she focused on it more, the pangs dulled and her blinding lust faded into a sweet passion. Her hunger subsided slightly as she relished in the recent memory.

The bed was soft beneath her hands and knees as she crawled onto it and waited for her lover. She could have slipped under the sheets or simply reclined back and waited for him with her golden, creamy thighs parted to welcome him in. No, she decided to give herself fully to him, to wait for him patiently and submissively, willing to let him take her as he wanted.

Then Donovan appeared at the doorway. His slender, muscled body took her breath away and she closed her eyes and dipped her head in submission. Her legs were slightly parted and her smooth back was arched, tilting her soft, silky ass up for him. Charisse could see the hunger in his eyes and felt the passion of his gaze as he drank in the angelic sight before him.

When his hands touched her hips and the tip of his throbbing manhood shallowly pierced her wet, waiting folds, she moaned wantonly. She could feel the love radiating from him and felt the heat of his flesh as he penetrated her slowly. His piercing drove her to a higher state, a plane full of passionate colors, and pure euphoria.

Charisse gave herself to him fully. The tenderness in which he touched her sent chills through her body. They moved in unison, determined and passionate, slow then faster, but gentle and intense all woven together in a mesh of love. She had never experienced the glow of true love-making. Then again, this was only the second time she had been with a man.

Donovan's hips moved in tight circles and brushed firmly against her tender rear. This was everything he wanted their first encounter to be but understood her unchecked hunger. He too had felt the pangs from the hidden, before he learned of his true nature. He too had unleashed his inner beast the first time he coupled with a woman. Perhaps that is why now, here in his bedroom with Charisse, he felt as vulnerable as her.

He shared her pain and desire, re-living his own ascendance to manhood as she bloomed into a woman. Donovan's eyes were wide open, locked on the woman writhing before him. He was dialed into her emotions and keen to her subtle keys. To him, they were the perfect pair, each undoubtedly knowing what the other wanted.

By now Charisse had forgotten about her shower and had resigned herself to the comfort of her bed. She loved herself as purely as Donovan had and though she wished her recollection of their love-making would last forever, she was already feeling the pull of her approaching climax.

Charisse fast-forwarded the interlude. Donovan's sweaty body was on top of her. Her glistening, smooth legs were wrapped around his tapered waist, urging him to love her harder and faster. Their eyes never left each other's throughout the moment. She could feel his enraged shaft pulsing hard deep inside of her as it grew bigger, cocking itself to release the culmination of their heat.

Her teeth gnashed into her lower lip as she arched her back and relived Donovan's sweet release. Charisse clenched her thighs together tightly as the tremors of her orgasm thundered through her body. She could still feel the heat of Donovan's seed as it pumped violently into her, dousing the flames of her desire into warm, smoldering satisfaction.

Spent from her reverie, Charisse wobbled to the shower and turned it off. She collapsed on her bed and gazed dreamily at the ceiling. Somehow Donovan was the key to controlling her intense hunger. She wondered if it were Donovan at all. Perhaps it was simply the love they shared. When she focused on their love-making, rather than their previous bout of raw, unbridled sex, she was able to control her urges. Charisse fell asleep with thoughts of Donovan swimming through her mind.

"Earth to Charisse," Frankie teased and snapped his fingers a few times.

Charisse blinked a few times and shifted her eyes to her father. His snorting laugh put a smile on her face. She was still caught up in the revelation she had last night and missed pretty much all of the one-sided conversations they were having.

"Sorry," she said. "Charisse here."

"Glad you made it back," Frankie quipped. "About yesterday, yeah, I'm sorry."

"I understand, dad," Charisse replied. She really did.

"But you know me. Matter-of-fact and I believe it's better to fix the situation immediately and completely rather than letting it spin out of control."

"Of course," she smiled deviously. "It also sends a very distinct message. Like preventive maintenance, eh?"

"Exactly," Frankie agreed.

He had been rather upbeat the last few weeks. He'd seen his daughter take more of an interest in their business and she didn't seem too faint of heart. There was no room for emotion or weakness when running an organization like this. The business was business. Frankie saw that everyone got their slice of the pie and took very good care of his people.

"Since you seem to understand where I'm coming from," he folded his hands on his desk and leaned back in his chair a bit. "I've got an important job for you."

Charisse's eyes seemed to sparkle in anticipation. She'd waited for a long time to see if she was really ready to carry on in her father's place. She felt she was getting there and hopefully whatever this job was, she'd prove it to him and to herself too.

ABOUT THE AUTHOR

Shala Breece is an emerging erotica author of many erotica kinks and sub-genres. Be sure to check out other books and leave a review if this story got you hot!

Visit my blog at Shala Breece Blog

Join my newsletter for exclusive Shala Breece Newsletter

Sign up for Free Stories from Xplicit Press Authors

Xplicit Press Author Updates

Like Xplicit Press on Facebook

Follow Xplicit Press on Twitter

Readers: I want to expand a few of the stories to see where the characters can be explored further. If there are any of the stories that you would like to read more about again, I'd love to hear from you!

Keep In Touch
Shala Breece
info@shalabreece.com